This

Matzah Ball Book

belongs to:

_____

_____

_____

Klutzy   Shmutzy

Kvetchy   Shluffy   Noshy

Shmutzy Girl

by Anne-Marie Baila Asner

MATZAH BALL BOOKS®

Shmutzy Girl lives in a shmutzy room,

With windows so shmutzy she can barely tell if it's night or day,

And her shmutzy toys piled on the floor.

Shmutzy Girl's parents make her close her bedroom door to keep the shmutz away from the rest of the house.

Some of Shmutzy Girl's clothes are so shmutzy that washing them doesn't get out the shmutz stains.

If her clothes happen to be clean at the beginning of the day, by the time she comes home they are always filled with shmutz.

Whether it's . . .

Lunch in the cafeteria,

Mud in the playground,

Or arts and crafts at school,

Shmutz clings to Shmutzy Girl like metal to a magnet.

Every day is a new adventure and every day brings more shmutz Shmutzy Girl's way.

It's not that Shmutzy Girl wants to be shmutzy.

For awhile, Shmutzy Girl tried to keep clean, but it took a lot of time and effort and it wasn't as much fun as eating and playing and making things her shmutzy way.

And really the only time Shmutzy Girl paid her shmutz much notice was when other people brought it to her attention,

"Don't you have anything less shmutzy to wear for your school picture?" asked her teacher.

"Shmutzy Girl, you left a ring around the pool!"
shouted the lifeguard.

Her shmutz didn't seem to bother her friends.

Shmutzy Girl still played ball with Klutzy Boy.

Shmutzy Girl still had slumber parties with Shluffy Girl.

One day, not too long ago, Shmutzy Girl went for a walk into town.

On her way home, she ran into Kvetchy Boy. Kvetchy Boy always complained, but that didn't stop Shmutzy Girl from saying "hello."

"Good day, Kvetchy Boy," Shmutzy Girl said with a smile and a spring in her step.

Kvetchy Boy grumbled, "Good day? Good day? My back is aching, the sun is too bright, my ice-cream is melting . . . Shmutzy Girl, what could you possibly know about a good day? Look at you. You're covered with shmutz!"

"Uh . . ."

"Uh . . ."

"You're right, Kvetchy Boy. I *am* covered with shmutz.
Pretty much from my head to my toes.

"But that doesn't mean I don't know a good day when
I see one," she said with her head held high.

"Good day, Kvetchy Boy."

Kvetchy Boy looked surprised.

Then he said, "Well then, uh, good day, Shmutzy Girl."

Shmutzy Girl continued on her way home to her shmutzy room, with windows so shmutzy she can barely tell if it's night or day and her shmutzy toys piled on the floor.

For the first time she understood that being shmutzy didn't make her good or bad, smart or dumb, happy or sad.

She would have a good day with or without it.

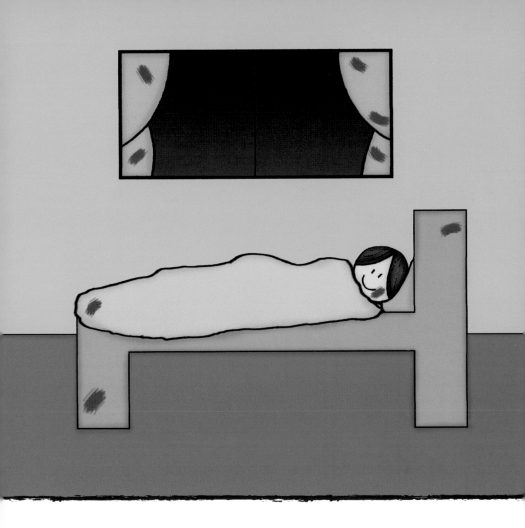

Shmutzy Girl is shmutzy.

It's the way she is . . .

And that's just fine.

Kvetchy   Shluffy   Noshy

Klutzy   Shmutzy

Glossary

A Bissle (little bit) of Yiddish

Bubbe (bŭ-bē) *n.* grandmother

Keppy (kĕpp-ē) *n.* head; *adj.* smart, using one's head

Kibbitzy (kĭbbĭtz-ē) *v. kibbitz* to joke around; *adj. kibbitzy*

Klutzy (klŭts-ē) *adj.* clumsy

Kvelly (k'vĕll-ē) *v. kvell* to be proud, pleased; *adj. kvelly*

Kvetchy (k'vĕtch-ē) *adj.* whiny, complaining

Noshy (nŏsh-ē) *v. nosh* to snack; *adj. noshy*

Shayna Punim (shā-nă pŭ-nĭm) *adj.* pretty *(shayna)*; *n.* face *(punim)*

Shleppy (shlĕp-ē) *v. shlep* to carry or drag; *adj. shleppy*

Shluffy (shlŭf-ē) *adj.* sleepy, tired

Shmoozy (shmooz-ē) *adj.* chatty, friendly

Shmutzy (shmŭtz-ē) *adj.* dirty, messy

Tushy (tŭsh-ē) *n.* buttocks, bottom

Zaide (zā-dē) *n.* grandfather

For information about Matzah Ball Books, visit

www.matzahballbooks.com

Products

◀ **toddler tee**
sizes: 2T & 4T

youth & adult tees ▶
sizes: S, M, L

◀ **infant set**

Noshy Boy dish set ▶

Shmutzy Girl dish set ▶

HOW TO ORDER:

- website: www.matzahballbooks.com
- e-mail: orders@matzahballbooks.com
- phone: (310) 306-7741